A New U

by Arthur Restham
illustrated by Becky Wilson Kelly

We need a new wheel.

Don't talk. Don't touch.

How about a big wheel?

A big wheel? No deal.

How about a small wheel?

A small wheel? No deal.

**How about
a tall wheel?**

A tall wheel? No deal.

How about a slow wheel?

A slow wheel? No deal.

How about a fast wheel?

A fast wheel? No deal.

How about a fancy wheel?

A fancy wheel? It's a deal!